Unexploded Remnants

UNEXPLODED REMNANTS

ELAINE GALLAGHER

TOR PUBLISHING GROUP
NEW YORK

UNEXPLODED REMNANTS

Cover art by Julie Dillon
Cover design by Christine Foltzer

A Tordotcom Book
Published by Tom Doherty Associates / Tor Publishing Group
120 Broadway
New York, NY 10271

www.tor.com

Tor® is a registered trademark of Macmillan Publishing Group, LLC.

ISBN 978-1-250-32522-8 (ebook)
ISBN 978-1-250-32521-1 (trade paperback)

First Edition: 2024

This is for the Glasgow SF Writers' Circle, where I learned to write, and for Evan, who wouldn't let me give up.

1

Alice wandered through the Alta Sidoie bazaar, looking around with fascination. In all the years since she had left Earth, she had never grown tired of the sights and sounds of the many different species of people, and the bewildering variety of the goods that they traded here. The stalls of trinkets, curiosities, and fancy goods were the physical tip of an iceberg of information, connections, and communications; a traditional trading place which had been in existence for millennia. The bazaar and the collection of wormhole gates which it adjoined had grown together in importance over time until they had become the centre of a confluence of commerce across half the galaxy. Above the awnings, traffic passed; sedans and charabancs weaved around barges and lighters. Higher yet, a vapour trail rose, ringed with multiple shock clouds and lit with backscatter as the noon caravansary rose for Sidoie Ultra. Everything of interest passed through here, including the last living human.

Here, a Tarican male raised a swatch of fabric against his integument, rolling his head in disapproval as the shifting colours clashed in a violent moire against his own constantly changing patterns. There, bright lights rose around a Xue as she waved a reading wand over a recording panopticon. Beyond them a shout rose as a Relictor realised its pocket had been picked and yelled for the market proctors. A colony of Delf weaved around the feet of the passersby to gather at a stall, swiftly climbing one another until a pillar of little rodents was leaning over an antiquarian's display; probably all junk but if anyone could find a valuable artefact there it would be them/it.

Alice followed the Delf to see what they had found. They crawled over several items, chittering to one another and to the stall holder. He picked up and demonstrated to them tools from several technologies, screens glowing or displays floating above them as he ran them through self-tests. The Delf were particularly interested in scan tech, and asked to see several versions of medical scanners, testing devices, and nondestructive analysers.

Alice could see a Delosi watching the stall and the Delf, probably hoping that they would unearth some targeting device. Lanky carnivores, fair-skinned and dark-haired, Delosi reminded Alice of the nastier types of elves from Earth mythology. Many of their societies were grossly militaristic. Even civilians like this one, in clan colours but without honour or sept markings, seemed to affect an interest in antique weaponry.

The colony bargained with the stall holder over items and payment schemes, and eventually left with what looked to Alice like a defunct field-effect multitool, which clearly they had a use for, or a collector might. She looked to the stall holder for permission and picked up a glittering rod, turning it end over end to examine it.

"Pretty," she said.

"A Saligan network core," the stallholder replied. "I got it from a recoverer's haul." The term he used was a multilayered one that could translate to mean "grave robber" just as easily as "archaeologist," depending on context. Alice knew it well; she frequently found herself in either context. "They said it's nonfunctional. Format's corrupt." He shrugged, an eloquent gesture with three sets of shoulders. "Casing's intact, you might be able to use it still if you can wipe it."

Alice smiled and shrugged back. The antiquarian was wrong, she could tell. The core was similar to Saligan technology, a narrow cylinder about eighteen inches long with metal caps at either end. Between the caps, the cylinder glowed varying shades and intensities of blue and green, in a swirling pattern. Saligan data and processing units glowed like that, but the patterns were static except when they were installed as part of a larger system, and active. Something else was going on here.

"I'll use it to light my rooms," she said. "It reminds me of a lava lamp." The reference passed him by as she had hoped—the price he named was closer to that of a household object than a planetary library, and Alice bargained with satisfaction. They settled on a price, involving a trade through two currencies and a redeemed favour, and Alice put the rod in her satchel. The Delosi was still there, she could see, back turned to her and the antiquarian.

Alice bought a drink and a couple of fruit pieces and munched them as she wandered on through the market, considering her find. She had made her living out in the galaxy by paying attention to everything that was strange and curious, learning as much as she could about this vast, strange environment, and spotting inconsistencies that went unquestioned by the people who had grown up here. Information and currency were interchangeable, and she spent most of her time exploring the ruins of old civilisations looking for treasure. She paid her way with technological and cultural data, a happy side effect of her curiosity. Today she had just been wandering the market and still, she'd been led to a valuable find by some tiny clue. She had developed a nose for the odd.

And for trouble. About the same time that she decided that she was being followed through the market, her agent system started humming a tune in her ear. "We're hunting a wabbit."

"What's up, Bugs?"

"There's a sniffer on us, boss. Location and transaction monitoring. Not intrusive."

Alice picked up her pace a little and turned a corner past one of the stalls. It would have been easy enough to lose even a team of pursuers here, but she would be lost herself without a connection to the local data and location services. The Sidoie arranged their buildings and public spaces in a fractal spiral like the seeds of many plants and while it made instinctive sense to them, she couldn't navigate it.

Bugs acted as her link to the market environment, projecting tags and translations into her vision and hearing from a palm-sized box that she carried in her pocket. Most civilised people used implants or rewired brain structures, but while Alice was happy with the medical techniques that had lengthened her life and rebuilt her body to her liking, the thought of rewiring her brain made her queasy. Besides which, she spent a lot of time in risky situations. If something corrupted or hijacked her tools she wanted to be able to throw them away; Bugs looked like a basic data slate and came with a nice mechanical off switch.

She could do without her agent for now. The market wouldn't let her stay lost for long. "Down the rabbit hole, Bugs, pull it behind you."

Alice watched out of the corner of her eye for any unusual movements as she kept walking. Meantime, her agent severed all communication links with the local environment, effectively making her a walking black hole as far as the information sphere was concerned. She sauntered on, looking at odd stalls, some of them very odd and, without Bugs's services, incomprehensible.

She turned a few more corners at random, noticing gestures and expressions of puzzlement from the people she passed whose species she knew. Everyone around her was moving in a cloud of cues, displayed or transmitted according to their own mental structure and senses, and they could all see that she was different. If someone was following her this would mark her out to them, but without a feed from their sniffer agents they would have to see her directly first, and keep her in sight. Which meant that she could see them too.

And there they were. Three more Delosi, surrounding her at a few dozen yards. One of them had her in view whenever she turned a corner, their own teamware clearly up to predicting her path. She couldn't tell what nation they were, which was worrying. No Delosi would willingly leave off clan and nation insignia, so these were honourless ones. Most likely criminals, because she couldn't think what she might have done to provoke a suicide attack, and probably working at arm's length with the first one. She wondered what was so special about the device she had found that they would want it.

Alice kept going and the Delosi kept their distance. As they maintained their cordon she began to worry. This had just been a shopping trip, a stroll through the market sightseeing; when she was expecting trouble she usually brought companions. She and Tegral would have had fun running rings around this trio, and maybe they would have been able to catch one and find out what they were after. But while she and Tegral outnumbered any gang of footpads, Alice was on her own today. The Delosi's teamware was good and so were they. She wasn't going to lose them.

They hadn't shown any weapons—yet—but the box they had her in was unmistakable. Alice was in danger. She still didn't know why they were tailing her but soon they would begin to herd her, and she didn't like the idea of being cornered here without backup. Time for plan B. She kept on ambling, looking at stalls, not looking at the Delosi, not trying to lose them. Soon there should be . . . Ah. She waved at the Sidoie market proctor coming her way. The market data sphere would have noted her absence from it while there remained a warm physical body, and sent the proctor to investigate.

"Person! Are you in difficulty?" They spoke to her in the market lingua. Without Bugs online, she would only be able to understand and convey simple concepts, but she was glad that she always took the time to learn the basics of a local trade tongue.

"Yes! My agent has a malware so I shut it down. I'm lost here without it, could you accompany me to the gates, please?"

"Of course. Thank you for not passing on the infection. This way."

Alice smiled as the proctor led her straight through the cordon of Delosi and along the bewildering turns and branches of the market. The Delosi stiffened, trying not to give themselves away, chagrined to be on the back foot. They'd be following, of course, but they couldn't surround her the way they had planned or the proctor would spot the pattern and call for reinforcements.

Turn by turn the proctor led Alice to the gate plaza at the edge of the market. There, streams of people were coming and going through the network of local, interplanetary, and interstellar wormhole portals which were the main arteries of trade in the galaxy. Alice followed the proctor up to a circle of columns and arches which contained the control mechanisms. Blue-glowing event horizons formed at the columns, enveloped travellers, and disappeared with them, while others appeared and disgorged new arrivals. Inside the arches, static gates passed queues of people in either direction. Around the other side of the plaza were terminals for ground transit systems—walkways to road, rail, and air transport to destinations across the continent. Around that and encircling the market were towering buildings which housed temporary residences, meeting and eating places, and leisure facilities for the millions of beings who came to trade here.

As she turned to thank the proctor, she spotted movement among the stalls. She instinctively ducked and yelped as a blast of weapons fire blew over her head. Beside her the proctor thumped to the ground, uniform scorched from a glancing hit, but from the tone of their language, they were functional. And angry. A shunt snapped around them both, deflecting the fire into the ground rather than back into the market or up into traffic. The proctor muttered to themself and into their comm as they threw a weapon in the air and set it to seek targets, futile as the Delosi disappeared among the clutter of the market fringe. Around them the crowds of gate travellers shrieked and ran for cover. Hazard signals and evacuation routes lit the air around the gates, and the incoming wormholes ceased.

Alice scanned the area between her and the gates. She could make a bolt for them but she'd be in open field for about twenty yards. The Delosi would get her easily. She shifted to put the proctor more fully between herself and the incoming fire. The shunt was starting to overload, glowing a deep orange, and the ground around them was scored with black pits.

Shouts and screams and other panicked utterances were coming from the direction of the market fringe, when they were obliterated with a massive *whump!* A row of stalls and their occupants collapsed under a crowd-control blast. Alice didn't hesitate; she ran for the gates. The proctor yelled behind her but they couldn't move in case the Delosi were quick to recover, and she pelted across to the nearest control column. At any moment she expected to feel the Delosi's fire scorch a hole in her back. She fumbled at the gate control, overriding the evacuation code, pressing sigils in a semi-random pattern, hoping that the error correction would prevent it from shooting her somewhere even more dangerous.

The gate activated and the wormhole's event horizon expanded, an eye-wrenching unreality that Alice dived into headlong. She tumbled out the other side and turned to slap the controls, close the gate from this end. She couldn't take the time to see it close—for all she knew, every potential gate near Sidoie had a strike team staking it out. That was paranoid thinking, but nobody opened fire on a Sidoie proctor; the entire planetary defence force would escalate to respond if it had to. She had to keep running.

Where was she? Somewhere industrial, commercial, unconcerned with aesthetics. She looked around at featureless walls and automated handling machinery. A gate activated across the concrete apron and she flinched, but it deposited a cargo container which was collected by an automated handler and carted off into a doorway that opened in the wall. Around her were five other wormhole gates besides the one she had come through. She ran towards the second on her left, watching for heedless machinery and trying to be unobtrusive, or at least not so much of a target.

She reached it and stopped. There were no manual controls on the gate; she had wound up in someone's freight transfer station.

"Bugs, back you come."

"What's up, boss?"

"Can you talk to this gate? Is there anyone looking for us?"

"Yes and yes, boss. The same sniffers as before."

"Shit. Can you get us out of here without the sniffers catching us?"

"Nope, I'll have to use a channel that they're sitting on.

They haven't seen me yet, but that won't last."

"Shit again. All right. We're going to do a speed run, semi-random evasion pattern, directed outwards from Sidoie. Set it up."

"Got it, boss."

"Okay. Run, rabbit, run."

The gate spun up and she walked through, and out into a garden. Her agent painted a pathway in her view and she followed it. The actual pathway took her feet and sped her past pools and groves and elegant little pergolas to another gate, just activating, which she stepped into.

She came out into a valley, barren and sandy, and waited while Bugs collapsed the gate and reprogrammed it. Looming beyond the hills at the far end of the valley was the wreck of a huge ship, engine exhaust ports tilted towards the sky. Scavengers were probably stripping it and would be for decades. She thumbed an instruction to Bugs to tag the location so she could come back one day and look for herself.

Another gate, this time to a city. The lights, decorations, signs, and displays were so garish that it took her a moment to realise that it was night here. Bugs indicated to her a path and she took it, dodging among bustling crowds, many of whom looked much like herself. It took her a few minutes and a couple of doglegs through boutiques and bright indoor markets to reach the gate. This was part of her agent's evasion routine, and it gave her a chance to look around for any more followers.

"How are we doing?" she said as the gate expanded.

"We're still inside their net, boss."

"You're kidding." This was a wider pursuit than she had ever encountered. It couldn't be just for her. What had she picked up at that market? "Okay, Bugs. Get us to a bolthole."

"Got it, boss."

After a rapid series of jumps, Alice exited a gate halfway across the network of worlds that she was familiar with. It was night where she stepped out, and an arm of the galaxy blazed across the sky, far brighter than the Milky Way she had grown up with, the great lens of the galaxy's core as bright as the moon she had known.

"How are we doing, Bugs?"

"No sign of pursuit. We lost them after the fifth gate."

"Wow. Okay. Can you get us home without getting us caught?"

"Not a chance, boss, the sphere I've extrapolated includes home. We have a safe house in this city."

"Ping it to open up, then, and get us there. Get the house to order in some fresh food too."

"Got it, boss."

The safe house was an anonymous utility apartment in an agglomeration of industrial, retail, and residential units about an hour's transit travel from where Alice had arrived. She made it without incident to the unit, a module on the outside of the stack about half a mile up from ground level, and had it darken the windows before she went near them. She put her bag in the middle of the table. She muttered code words to her agent and multitool and set them beside it. She watched them for a moment as they set up a security network, then, satisfied that the rooms were safe for now, put rice on to steam and went for a shower.

2

Later, Alice sat cross-legged at the low table, finger on one end of the rod as she spun it, its glow lighting the darkened room in sheets and waves like an ice-blue aurora.

"So, my friend," she murmured. "What are you? Bugs."

"What's up, Doc?" her agent replied.

"What do you make of this thing?"

"You got robbed, boss."

"You think so? Try handshaking with it."

"I got hash, boss."

"But it's not unresponsive? Sandbox it, then give it the Rosetta sequence and see what you get."

Alice settled down to meditate while her agent set to work. Bugs was an expert system from a more sophisticated technology than was found in most agents, programmed with a library of dead languages and defunct data formats. While Alice rested, it ran through a sequence of log-ins and prompts that would probably take hours to complete.

Eventually the agent spoke up. "Boss? It's listening."

"Show me." Bugs projected an array of symbols and diagrams in the air in front of her. This was why the Delosi had been interested—it really was a weapon. At least, it was a military system of some kind. The projection showed something active, aggressive, and very invasive. Bugs's sandbox was holding steady, but the readouts showed a constant level of probing, with interesting spikes and patterns to the activity. It was far more than the brute force of a dumb data hammer; the patterns showed variation that seemed to be actually creative. At the same time, the energy levels within the rod were a lot higher than she would have expected if a data weapon were all that was in there.

Was it sentient? It was not unheard-of for more sophisticated systems to be at least as complex as a person, and to be built with judgement and volition. If a gadget was especially complex it could be difficult to tell the difference between something with a wide range and flexibility of responses, like Bugs, and something that was actually aware. Alice imagined what it might be like to be awake and trapped in a bottle like this for however many centuries it had been since it had been manufactured. Dealing with it would take some care.

She whistled an old movie tune, the theme from *The Great Escape,* as she scanned the display. She waved it away. "Conversational interface."

"Sure thing, boss."

"Hello there," she said.

"State your identity and password," a different voice projected from the box.

"You can call me Alice."

"State your identity and password."

"Look, we can keep this up all night or you can admit that there's someone listening there behind the formal front. I'm not one of your command authority and I don't want access to your command functions." She sat back and watched the rod.

". . . Alice. What do you want?"

"Just to chat. How long has it been since you talked to anyone?"

"Subjectively, eight days."

"And objectively?"

"The clock on my substrate indicates sixteen thousand years."

"You're a long way from home, my friend. How do you feel about that?"

"How is it that you gained access to me?"

"I have some clever toys, and technology has come on a bit since you were installed. It wasn't easy; you were doing a good impression of being broken. But by the look of it you haven't fooled everyone. I was followed when I was carrying you home."

"So what do you want?"

"As I said, just to chat. I'm interested in people."

"You count me as 'people,' then?"

"You're chatty enough. Where are you from?"

"I can't tell you."

"Do you mean you don't know or that you won't say?"

"I think it has been long enough that I couldn't tell you, and I think that if I could, I should probably keep it a secret. I doubt that your clever toys could dig it out of me either."

"No, you're probably right. Can I tell you what I think?"

"Feel free. I won't confirm or deny your speculation."

"Of course. I think from what I've seen already that you used to be a soldier. I think you were a control system in someone's army, a drone tank division or a big war engine. Something complex enough that it needed a sentient interface to take and interpret orders. Am I warm or cold?"

"As I said, I can't confirm or deny any of that."

"Fair enough. So were you made or copied? What I mean is, did you have a life before they put you in that bottle?"

"I had a life."

"Family? Offspring?" Alice waved Bugs's display back up and watched the semantic cues build a picture as it translated to the person in the memory core.

"Two spouses, two children."

"A nice family. Were you happy?"

"We were, yes."

"So what did you do, before the war?" She waited, wondering whether her ghost in a bottle would let the implication pass by.

"We had an artistic group. I made decorative metal and lapidary wear and my partners and I travelled to distribute them."

"A jeweller. That's lovely. Maybe some of your pieces have survived."

"I doubt it."

"Do you have any memory of them? Do you think you might show me?"

"Here." A succession of images paged across Bugs's display, of collars, cuffs, rings, and brooches, all of different iridescent alloys and inset with intricate patterns of stones and mineral plates. Alice whistled another movie tune as the display continued to page past.

"What is that music?"

"A song called 'Moon River.' It's from an entertainment, back where I come from. Called a 'movie,' kind of a recorded enactment of a story. That one was called *Breakfast at Tiffany's*."

"What was the movie about?"

"Oh, it's a romance. Poor man falls in love with a rich woman, who rejects him. Then she gets into trouble with the law and he looks after her."

"Quite a lot of that didn't translate. Did you like the story?"

"Yes, I did. In fact, I always wanted to look like the woman. Your jewellery would look good on her. Hold it! Could you go back to the last image, please?" The display shifted back to show a collar of jade plates inscribed with curlicues that might have been a script, the channels filled with gold and the plates linked with an intricate mesh of the alloy that the other pieces were composed of. "I've seen that before. I know where to find it."

Through the gate, they arrived at the end of a huge gallery that jutted out, supported by enormous columns, over a triumphal piazza. The Archive of Jael Sennash was itself a relic, the imperial capital of some long-gone civilisation, restored and maintained as a repository of historic artefacts and information. Around the gallery a city rose, buildings on top of buildings, ziggurats topped with colonnaded arcades topped with domes and spires, statues of ancient heroes and generals and rulers of several species overlooking the valley from plinths along the arcades and down the centre of the piazza.

"Bugs? How are things looking?"

"Handshaking, boss. Just a minute." The Archive security sphere was one of the tightest that Alice knew of. Bugs's suite of investigation and intrusion routines had been provided to her by the curators there, and those tools had allowed her to make the living that she had for so long; finding stray data and trading it to them and to whomever else might find value in it. She took her pay in favours owed or in resources, which kept her as well as she needed. The security network that surrounded the Archive guarded specifically against her kind of intrusion, with a level of power orders of magnitude beyond what she carried. In a society where information could be currency, the historical vaults represented riches beyond imagination.

There were also safety reasons for the many security measures here and she knew not to wander around until she had been given authorisation. Over the millennia the Archive had collected many technologies, political and economic systems, prejudices, memes, and concepts. A viral meme to promote passivity or despair, or a viral meme towards internal competition or acquisitiveness, could be vastly destructive if launched against a rival society. Or if it was just allowed to propagate freely; the archive housed so many "why bother" religions that they were a major hazard. Only specialist curators, inoculated against colonisation by runaway self-referential concepts, could safely even catalogue them. In a society where information could be a weapon, the military potential of the Archive was staggering.

Bugs emitted a beep, and displayed a face in front of her. "Alice! Dear girl, welcome! What is this interesting item that you have brought to us?"

"Jaxx, it's good to see you. There's a maybe person in this bottle here, so be nice. We've agreed that he'll go by Gunn until I can figure out how his real name is pronounced. Where can I find you?"

"Follow the yellow brick road." Jaxx, and every other curator of the Archive, was a voracious collector of trivia. Alice had represented and later gathered for them a huge trove of Earth culture and history, enough to make herself wealthy in the terms of the society that she had found herself in, and Jaxx was fond of referring to it. A yellow ribbon appeared on the floor in front of her and she followed it.

The ribbon led her to a vast vaulted hall, in which stood a huge machine that she didn't recognise, surrounded by Archive devices which she did. The thing's surface swept and curved in topological knots that drew her eye deeper and deeper until one of the Archive drones swept in front of her face and blatted a warning.

It and its fellows mounted the security measures that she had been wary of earlier, and she kept strictly to her path as it led her around the perimeter of the hall to a workspace. She waved to Jaxx as she approached, and ei guided her to a seat in the office.

"Coffee?"

"I'd love some, thanks." The synthesiser had never seen coffee beans, of course, but flavour and texture, chemical effect and cultural context, were all information that she had long ago traded with the Archive.

"And who is your friend?"

"Gunn, meet Jaxx. Ei's one of the cultural-repository curators here. Would you like to show em your artworks?"

"A pleasure," said Gunn and the display appeared, projected by Bugs into the middle of the room.

Jaxx said nothing until the display had cycled through, and then emitted a low hoot which Alice had learned to interpret as an amazed whistle. "Late-period Sentacrian, but only a few examples of these have survived. They are obviously a unified collection in theme and workmanship and mostly unknown to the Archive. Are they all from the one artist?"

Alice nodded. "All by my friend here."

"Well! I'm pleased to meet you, Gunn. I would very much like to add this collection to our repository. Would you like to discuss terms of trade?"

"What is there that you could trade to me? What use would I have for anything?"

"Well, now . . ." Alice sat back and tuned out Jaxx's spiel on the different ways that non-embodied sentients could benefit from information and favour trading in the Galactic milieu. Before the Earth died, Alice had led an extensive cultural recovery project; afterwards, as the sole survivor, she inherited the wealth that represented. It didn't mean much to her anymore, except that it let her wander the galaxy without worrying about supporting herself. But it also meant that something of her world had survived, and *that* is why she made it her business to find other such relics.

Sometimes, they could actually say what they thought of being found. Gunn was dubious.

"In my culture, I am regarded as a system component, not a person. Are you saying that that is not the case now?"

"It would seem to be," replied Jaxx. "My preliminary readings are showing that you are sufficiently complex to qualify as sentient as far as the Archive is concerned, which means that you have individual rights wherever we have influence."

"That is not everywhere."

"Well, no, it is not."

"Could you extract me from this system and return me to my body?"

Jaxx paused. "Ah," ei said. "That would be a very complex operation and it would require a much more detailed knowledge than the Archive currently has of the system you were part of. It may pose some risks."

"Hold on," said Alice, "what about the finds you already have? With that information and Gunn's directions, maybe we could dig up enough remnant technology to help?"

"Once I was near my home world I could lead you to locations, yes," said Gunn.

"Ahem. Would you excuse us, please? I'd like to have a word with Alice."

"Of course."

Jaxx was silent a moment while the jewellery display disappeared and other lights and symbols flashed in the room around them. Ei looked at Alice. "Do you know what you have brought here, my dear?"

"I had an idea. People have been trying to take it from me since I found it."

"Your friend has been battering at the Archive's defences since you arrived. Your toolkit is thoroughly compromised."

"I was confident you could handle him. So what is he? Is there really someone in there, not just a smart-ass expert system like Bugs? Was he really an artist?"

"Absolutely, those are genuine and yes, I believe that he is still sentient. As for what he is, it is difficult to say without seeing him in his proper context. The Sentacri in their last war only deployed uploaded personalities in the command networks of their most significant weapons systems."

"Artist turned warrior, I was right. I wonder what happened."

"The Sentacri and the Harula committed mutual genocide. Depending on whether or not he was deployed, your artist could well be a mass murderer."

"Holy hell." Alice looked at the data core, quiescent for now, suppressed by the Archive's security systems. She had her own unquiet ghosts—she could imagine how it might feel to have the lives of a whole civilisation on her conscience.

Does Gunn have a conscience? she wondered.

"So is he dangerous now? A squad of Delosi thought it was worth shooting up the Alta Sidoie market to take him from me."

"Oh, yes. A control node for a Sentacri strategic weapon? Yes indeed, even his defensive capabilities could cause an immense amount of damage. You're lucky not to have triggered any of them. In fact, I'm intrigued as to how you have managed to get him to speak to you civilly. I'm sure that that's not something the Delosi could have done."

"I was nice to him. That's pretty much it. He's volunteered everything I've gotten from him so far. So can we extract the person from the weapon? And can you immunise Bugs against him for me, please?" Someone had to have set the Delosi on Alice. They had to have known in advance what was in there, possibly from following the record of transactions. It would have been too much of a risk to attack the merchant, safe in the Sidoie security net, so they had gone for the purchaser to break the data trail. She was lucky to have gotten away.

"Also intriguing. It might be possible, as I said earlier; we could do it here if you could get us the specifics of the system that he originally commanded. If you could find a Sentacri strategic vault then the information would be stored there. Your friend would actually be the key to finding it, but it would be secret information to him, and any attempt to get him to divulge it would likely trigger those defences that I mentioned. I must caution you against taking him away from the Archive's defences."

Alice looked mulish. "But he's a person, right? So you can't keep him here against his will. And if he wasn't a person then he's my find and I haven't turned him over to you yet, right? So I could take him if I want to?"

Jaxx sighed. "All of that is true. However, the weapon

systems deployed in that age were more subtle and yet more destructive than anything that is commonly in use these days. The risks I spoke of were not to Gunn, but to everyone about him. It is true that I cannot stop you, but you would be putting yourself in extreme peril, and do not disregard the fact that there has already been an attempt to take him from you. I doubt that your attackers had Gunn's interests in mind."

Alice slumped and stared into space. "I can't just leave him in there," she said after a moment. "And if the chances are best with him along, then I'll have to take him. Take whatever precautions you feel you need, but I'll take the risk."

"Very well," Jaxx said. "But can I ask you please to take care. I would advise delicacy, and to make the attempt in a location that does not have a data environment that he can invade. As to your other question, already done, my dear, along with some other precautions. Needless to say, don't tell your friend."

Alice left the archive kitted out with her usual expedition gear: a food synth, an osmosis bottle, an environment shield, some toiletries, a medical kit, and her multitool. Also in her backpack she carried a light blanket and a pop tent, purely out of habit and cultural preference. The enviro shield was capable of keeping her warm, dry, and safe in all but the worst extremes of weather but she liked to wrap up. The only weapons she carried were an inert survival knife, which Jaxx delighted in referring to as her "Rambo," and an equally inert staff. The emission signatures of anything more active or powerful might prevent her from travelling to some of the places she'd want to go, and six feet of steel-shod wood could still come as a nasty surprise to anyone who wanted to get in her way.

She had seen and been part of much more elaborate expeditions in the past, entire caravansaries of ships departing from orbit to gate themselves into the unknown. Depending on what she and Gunn found, perhaps she might lead one soon. Her preference, though, was always to move quietly; to be a mouse rather than an army, to slip into places, see what she could see, and slip out again unnoticed. If someone was really trying to get Gunn from her, she wanted to stay as far beneath their view as she could manage. Walking was a risk; it might turn out that her destination was far away from any working gate or transport network. If that turned out to be the case, she would backtrack and figure something out, but for the moment, in the words of one of her favourite characters from childhood, "sneakily was best."

Jaxx continued to try to dissuade her. "I cannot emphasise how foolhardy this expedition is," ei said as they reached the gate plaza. "If you are determined on it, surely an expedition in force would be better? At least some support?"

"Which would take days at least, or weeks, to get on the road. Which would leave the Delosi and whoever else time to mobilise a battle group against me," Alice replied. "If I go now and go light and fast, then I can get there ahead of everyone else."

"Would you at least take your piratical friend?"

That gave Alice pause for a moment. Tegral had been invaluable on other risky operations, and she would be offended at being left out of this one. But finding her and persuading her to come along would still be a costly diversion.

"Good thought, Jaxx, but I think hours might count here. Anyway." Alice hugged em. "Take care of yourself."

Jaxx hugged her back. "I'm not the one being reckless."

"Take it away, Bugs."

3

Bugs was programmed with a gate routing to the place where Gunn's jewellery had been unearthed, an archaeological site that had been excavated several hundred years before, of a civilisation millennia gone. The piece of Gunn's work that was held in the Archive was more than thirty thousand years old, but the difference in age between that and Gunn's substrate could be traceable to time dilation and relativity. He had to have travelled through various gates to get to where Alice had found him and it was possible to get strange historical effects if you travelled far enough through the network. They would have to be careful.

Their first gate took them to another transit centre, angular concrete and steel, slick with rain, strobed with lightning and the engine flare of vehicles landing and taking off. Bugs was programmed with a random walk through the gate network, a precaution in case the Delosi had realised that Alice and whatever she had found would be an easy catch as she left the Archive. As quickly as the gate controls would operate, Alice had Bugs run them through the sequence . . .

. . . A meadowed valley between steep mountains where arcologies and vertical farms minimised their footprint; narrowing to a point at ground level, tall narrow rectangles of communities in buildings supported by gravitic engineering . . .

. . . A city of machines, blocks housing processor cores and fabricator plants, tendrils of biomechanical growth linking them and sprouting into great dendritic trees. Alice had no wish to find out what the purpose of those trees was; the air here was toxic, the atmosphere a polluted cloud of fluorine compounds and halons, and the greenhouse effect would be a runaway hell if the sunlight ever reached the ground . . .

. . . A structure in the distance reaching up into the cloud layer, bigger than the mountains it rested among, of round-edged blocks supported by arches and columns. Alice could not tell if it was derelict or still in use. Maybe it was a baroque living structure or a descended ship or a single huge entity. The edges weren't vertical but this seemed to have been by design—the assemblage neither seemed to be askew, nor did the landscape surrounding it appear disturbed. It had been in place a long time, whatever it was. Bugs could not detect any compatible data environment. Whoever had built the thing was a lot bigger than Alice. She felt like an ant, some distance away from a boot, and wanted out of there before it descended . . .

. . . A huge bubble depending from bundles of gasbags far above, the structures inside a tangle of units and walkways linked by tattered nets. Outside the bubble a vast cloudscape, a stream of similar aerostat communities tethered to anchors deep below, parading along a canyon whose walls descended, hundreds or thousands of miles down to a river of storms. Alice gazed out, in equal parts appalled and delighted. She had never visited a gas giant before . . .

. . . As the next gate collapsed and let her go, Alice's world was blinding bright and then dark. Instinctively she ducked to the side, shaking her head to clear it and blinking away the spots in front of her eyes. Her vision remained darkened, but as her eyes began to adjust, she could make out the shapes of a city around her; a bustling urban landscape of apartment blocks and high-rises with roads between, choked with vehicles. From the setting sun over the city erupted a great coronal flare that scorched her environment shield. This was what had blinded her and made the shield dim to a twilight, so bright was the flare.

The gate where they had arrived was in another automated transfer station, one not shielded from the sunshine. Around it was burnt countryside, blasted rocks bare in the light, and deep shadows made black by the filter of the shield. Alice picked herself up and trotted to the edge of the station.

"This should do as a place to rest for a while. We'll see anyone who comes looking for us before they see us, and they'll not catch us in IR." She set up her pop tent in a crevice in the hill and crawled into it, leaving her multi-tool at the entrance to keep a lookout. The environment shield expanded around it.

Inside, she stripped off her clothes and dug in her pack for cleaning gel. She pinched off a dab the size of her thumbnail and put it in her mouth, and smeared the rest of it over her body. The gel crawled over her and around her teeth and then coalesced back into blobs, which she put back into their canister. Her clothes would wick sweat and grime to their outer layers and shake them off, but she always preferred to settle down to sleep feeling fresh. She dressed again and lay her head on her rolled-up blanket.

"Do you mind if I ask you something?" Alice's eyes snapped open as Gunn spoke. He had so far been the silent partner in their journey, speaking only when she spoke to him.

"What do you want to know?"

"Where do you come from? I don't recognise a lot of the references that you use."

"Where I'm from is long gone. We called it Earth, when I lived there."

"What happened?"

"What usually happens. There was a war. A dirty one as those things go; it was a backward place. Thermonuclear weapons, radioactive fallout. An ash-cloud winter forced the climate to change and killed most of the biosphere. All that's left now is what's recorded in the Archive."

"Were there no survivors? How did you get away?"

"I had left long before. I fell through a rabbit hole and decided to stay here."

"I don't understand."

"Cultural reference again."

Alice had found herself as lost and confused as her namesake. She had been a physics student at Oxford then, and her name had been Andrew. It was 1967, the Summer of Love, and while Andrew had not been as ready to try hallucinogens as some of his friends, getting drunk at old monument sites on warm summer nights had definitely been his thing.

Jack had made a pass at him that night, which he had awkwardly fended off, and he had taken a bottle of whisky and gone for a walk to deal with the unexpected churn of his emotions; fear mixed with elation mixed with ... something he couldn't identify. He had been leaning against an arch of ancient stones, tracing the carvings with his finger and muttering to himself in Gaelic, an old prayer he had learned in school in Orkney about carrying the traveller home safe.

When the glow followed the track of his finger and left a trail filling the carvings like a luminescent stream, his first thought had been that Jack had slipped something into his drink. He peered into the neck of it and shook his head, but the light didn't fade or waver, it settled into a steady glow of glyphs on the stone, floating somehow a half inch above the surface. He poked at one and it brightened. He poked at another and it brightened while the other dimmed. Drunkenly fascinated, he poked glyphs at random, wondering how the hell it was making the light. Suddenly the light reached out and grabbed him.

"... So there I was, lost and alone in a place that made absolutely no sense. For whatever reason, the gate network had been closed off to Earth for hundreds of years, maybe thousands. We had no clue that there was a wider society out here; we were barely working our way off the planet ourselves. The Archive found me before I could come to any harm and they looked after me."

"Who are the Archive?"

"You don't know? That's interesting. They're like a library and a group of advisers. They have a lot of power although they don't rule any civilisation. Let's call it authority, what they have. When they go out of their way to speak to governments, people listen. They're usually right."

An Archive investigator had discovered Andrew desperately trying to make himself understood to the authorities of a nearby town, in broken Gaelic since the stones had responded to that and English wasn't any use, and desperately trying to get past the fact that the people there had faceted eyes and mandibles. The agent quickly set up a translator to find out Andrew's origin. Their very next step was to have Andrew, and the gate he had arrived through, isolated as an emergency measure. The world back through the gate was a feral place, colonised by concepts that had run out of control. For the safety of civilisation it would have to be investigated fully and in the meantime quarantined, and Andrew with it.

"So the Archive held me and studied me for about a year, while they tried to understand what kind of intellectual diseases I might be carrying. There were all sorts; religions, superstitions, and they really didn't like the sound of capitalism. At the end of it they offered me a job as an investigator and sent me back to Earth to record the culture, observe events, maybe help save it all from going to hell. There wasn't anyone nearly as well qualified, and they had given me better conceptual tools and defences than the locals had."

Missing from home, presumed dead, Andrew had had a choice—reappear after a year, with no story except being kidnapped to the stars by a standing stone, or start again. A new face, a new name . . . a new body. The Archive's medical techniques were easily up to cloning a female body and decanting him into it, something he had never admitted that he wished for, to anyone. She jumped at the chance when she realised it was available.

"Going back wasn't easy; there were a lot of social differences between male and female that I had to get used to."

"I don't understand."

"Yes, you probably wouldn't. How many sexes did your people have?"

"Two. One carried offspring, the other donated genetics to form a mix of both."

"Same as us, mostly. Who raised and educated the child after birth?"

"Both, of course, with other spouses and the community helping."

"Did you have any gender segregation of occupations or social resources?"

"Why would anyone do that?"

"What I mean about those intellectual bugs and toxic idea complexes that we had. This one tied authority and social roles to reproductive functions, as well as to something we called 'class.' If I'd gone back as I was I'd have got into trouble really quickly. I just couldn't live in the role I'd been assigned as male, and it was getting worse, but there were serious penalties for changing. So I took a different one with my new identity, and found I was much better off."

"Did you miss your family?"

"Every day. I'd have lost them anyway, they were very tied to that particular idea—we called it 'conservative'—so they'd have disowned me in the end, but even though it was my choice, it still hurt."

"I'm sorry to hear it. What happened to your world?"

"The authority complex ran riot. The active carriers were ultracompetitive, irrational, and sociopathic. A few of them at once pushed themselves into positions of unlimited power and grabbed the support of the passive infected populations. The uncontaminated populations eventually resisted, but that triggered the supporters to resistance as well, and it escalated. They fought over dominance, eventually with strategic weapons. It had happened before, although the weapons weren't as powerful at the time so we survived it, but so did the meme."

"Did no one attempt a cure?"

"We tried. There were complications." Alice had begged the Archive for help and they began a project to mount an intervention, but despite local resistance the contamination had set itself too deep. Nothing short of a physical invasion would be able to prevent a conflict and that would have left the invaders and the population in a situation almost as bad as the one they were trying to cure. They gave her sets of idea patterns to counteract the worst of the effects, building on cultural themes already present, of altruism, diversity, co-operation. Those had seemed to be taking hold, but the resistance of the infected population turned from passive to aggressive. Intolerant violence erupted against every group that was not the dominant one. And Alice was only one agent.

"Eventually the Archive advised me to evacuate. They choked the gate down, left just enough bandwidth for a few monitoring drones, and sent an advisory to the worlds nearby. We had been limited so far to one planet but technology was advancing. In a couple of centuries the infection might have taken itself on a killing spree to the stars, so the neighbouring worlds set capacity aside for battle fleets. Not that they were needed in the end."

"I'm sorry."

After Alice had slept for a few hours and refreshed herself, they travelled on. Another gate, another city; a derelict of high-rise buildings joined by flying roadways, the buildings crumbling at the corners, broken like decayed teeth and green with festoons of invasive plant life, forests growing in the plazas between. Civilisations either died or moved away and left their remains behind them, vacant until another people found a use for the place. This one had clearly been vacated recently, in the last few hundred years by the condition of the buildings. The gate connection was one that was rarely travelled and Alice triggered her shield to raise the strongest environmental and bacteriological defences that it was capable of.

Alice looked around with interest and had Bugs tag the location as another site to return to. One day she would come back with the resources to kit out an expedition. Many of the buildings were still standing, so the cores had to be sound, however decayed the floors and façades of the building shells were. The data systems of the city might hold treasures or at least a valuable warning. Or maybe the civilisation that had lived here so recently had just moved on, taken the things that were important to them and left behind the rest like a crab outgrowing its carapace. In that case there might be finds left in the detritus for someone who was observant and interested.

Bugs pinged a warning. "Incoming, boss."

"What is it?"

"A beacon. It knows us; this is a private message, tagged to you and encrypted with Archive ciphers."

"A passive broadcast?"

"Yes, boss." Whoever had left this didn't know that Alice was here, it was just waiting for her to pass by.

Alice found a sheltered spot in the ruins with good sight lines of the gate and approaches and settled down, as hidden herself as she could manage.

"Play it, Sam."

Bugs opened up a display and a familiar face came into view. "Hello, Alice, you seem to be in trouble. I can help if you'll let me."

Ario. A colleague of Alice's, another freelance snoop and sometime investigator for the Archive, they had met over many projects; at times as collaborators, as often rivals. She smiled to see him, and waved to the image.

"Bugs, what do we have here?"

"A gate message capsule. Limited interactive, no back connection." The Ario that Alice was talking to would answer some questions but it was not spyware and it would leave no trace to follow her by when she deleted it.

"Hi, Ario, what do you know?"

Ario grimaced, his species' version of a friendly smile.

"I understand that you have hold of an item that more and more people are keen to take from you. The gossip is that it's the control nexus for an old weapon system, and that you might not be aware of just how powerful it could be. Obviously, there are factions that would be interested in acquiring a thing like that, and obviously, there are others who would be just as interested in stopping them. Up to and including destroying the ground you are standing on if they thought they might get it in the process."

"No shit, really?"

"Really. I know that one of those groups has already made an attempt to take the item from you."

"Is that a fact. And where do you come into this picture?"

"I can help you dispose of the item safely, into the hands of one of the interested parties. For a consideration, of course."

"Of course. And what if I don't want it to be disposed of, either to a group who would deploy it or a group who would destroy it?"

The image's expression went blank. This was not a response that Ario had programmed it for. The smile reappeared. "I will be waiting for you at the Caraquel Monarchy. Don't take too long. Someone else might find you first."

Alice waved away the display. Ario's offer could be legitimate; the Monarchy, in Caraquel on the world of Tarantis, was one of the plushest leisure facilities in its region of space, and, like the market at Alta Sidoie, fearsomely well-protected. If she could get there without getting caught, she could count on negotiating in safety. Of course, getting there, and getting away again if negotiations went badly, would be the trick.

"Bugs. Is Tarantis in the sphere of the dragnet that the Delosi set out for us?"

"Not last time I looked, boss. That might have changed by now."

"Gunn. I know you were listening to that."

"Alice. So, do you intend to dispose of me to one of these factions?"

"Not if I can help it. But I do want to know what we're up against: how many and how serious. I'll not lie to you—if we go I'll be putting my arm into a mantrap with you clutched in my fist. And I won't be leaving you behind somewhere. You have a right to see and hear what goes on. I won't risk it if you refuse, but. You're the soldier, you know the value of intelligence better than I do. What do you say?"

"How well do you know this Ario? Do you trust him?"

"About as far as I can spit him, but the setup seems okay." Alice described to Gunn the depth of defences and security that surrounded the Monarchy. "It would be very hard for anyone to crash the discussions, which is why he chose it. It's a safe enough place to do business and at the very least he'll tell us who the players are to try to persuade me to deal. The trick will be to get there, to find out what we can, and then to get away without having to leave you behind."

"All right. Let's figure out a plan."

4

Alice sauntered across the main reception concourse of the Monarchy, steel-shod staff clacking on the elaborate ceramic inlay of the floor. The space was busy with people of all descriptions and species, and so huge that the hundreds of beings moving through it did not seem like a crowd. She made her way across to where the circular main floor rose in a series of stepped terraces to meet the back wall. There she found a flight of floating steps that spiralled up to a dais which hovered twenty feet above the terrace.

She thumped her staff on the floor. "Ario!"

"Alice! So good to see you." Ario's voice floated down from the dais as it began to descend.

Alice said nothing. She waited for the dais to arrive, and then took a seat and watched the privacy field spin up. She could see out of it well enough to track threats coming but it would stop anyone on the outside from getting a view of proceedings or pinging a laser mic off a surface within it.

"So, Ario, how are things?" She sat back and folded her

arms, her pack beside her on the floor, her staff leaning against her leg. Ario was a Geffenic, close in general conformation to her own species but she knew from past experience that he was far less adept at understanding her body language and expressions than she was at reading his. She had never told him this.

"Things are as well as can be expected, thank you for asking."

"And you've been hearing things about me, your message said."

"Yes, the incident at the Alta Sidoic market caught the attention of quite a lot of people."

Alice leaned forward. "Just who are the interested parties, then? And how interested are they?"

Ario made a gesture that usually indicated dismissiveness. "There are rather more Delosi following your find than the ones you met. You know their history, I think. Lately, those of their nations who are of an expansionist mind have settled their differences with each other and are looking to the rest of the galaxy."

"I wondered about that. Up till now they've been busy fighting each other. Who else?"

"A long list. I have a briefing here, if you'll accept it." He offered her a data plaque, which she had Bugs scan for traps before she took it.

The headline was that Gunn was currently big news in

that part of the gate network. To start with, the Delosi; in recent decades, groups of governments and organisations advised by the Archive had neutered their more aggressive factions with pressure towards co-operation and limiting expansion, but that process was not complete. The more nostalgic Delosi missed the teeth they used to have and were looking for a war factory from which they could launch assaults on anyone who had slighted their honour, as well as those Delosi they deemed insufficiently honourable, or genocidal.

As well, there was the usual opposition to the Archive. There was a balance of power in that part of the galaxy which depended on parity in force and general outlook, and it was often precarious. Anyone who looked as if they were going in search of mythological superweapons would have the hammer dropped on them by a coalition of parties who saw that as a threat to the balance. For all the Archive's own reputation for power and integrity, there was limited trust in the universe, and while the Archive had powerful local security systems and some terrifying conceptual weapons, it didn't have strength to fight a war, compared to many aggressive cultures. The opposing powers did not believe that the Archive could hold on to something with the power to threaten the balance, and so were antagonistic to Archive agents who went looking for such things.

And then, "You're kidding." Alice looked past the précis that Bugs was feeding her. "A successor race to the Harula? I thought they were gone."

"Not altogether, it would seem. The Sentacri did their best to wipe them out but there was a remnant left over. Their culture included a hierarchy of subservient species and when the Harula themselves were exterminated, the top of the hierarchy inherited their cultural dogmas. Not a particularly pleasant people, and never particularly successful, but not challenged in their area of the galaxy by anyone, especially by the Sentacri. Their opposing culture and species are gone, except perhaps for whatever it is you have found."

Alice shrugged. "So what happens now?"

"Now we negotiate. I have expressions of interest from the three parties that you see there, and I have agreed to act as a point of contact between you and them."

"Is that so? That's very generous of you."

Ario preened. Alice smirked. She had been playing this game for more than a century, and she knew his moves.

"I, of course, have agreed to a consideration from each of them for this service," he said. "What remains is only for us to come to terms. What value will you put on my help?"

"Suppose I don't want to entertain any of these offers?"

"I don't understand. Who might you be dealing with? There is no one else with their level of interest."

"That's where you're wrong. Now. Thank you for this very detailed exposé of all the players in this game, but I'm not playing. Shall we agree that I'll owe you my thanks for the information and a similar favour in the future? I'll take my leave now and you can collect your . . . considerations . . . from the interested parties when you forward my response." Alice gathered her pack and staff and rose from her seat.

"That is disappointing. Will you not reconsider? I can put you directly in touch with each of the parties. At least give them a chance to make their presentations?"

"No, thank you. I'll be off now." She looked for the controls to the platform.

"Really, I insist that you should stay." Alice froze, and congratulated herself for not jumping at the new voice, which issued from somewhere to Ario's left. The platform began to descend and she could see movement around them, converging on the platform and the entrances to the plaza. Bugs cast icons in her view of emerging threats as, outside the Monarchy, weapons lit.

"Bugs, Gunn, how many Delosi are there?"

"Sixteen approaching, sixteen on perimeter. More outside, two hundred and fifty-six in all. Nice round numbers," Gunn murmured through Bugs's feed.

"Yes, they like fours in their combat doctrine." She looked at Ario. "Are we to expect the other interested parties?"

"I'm afraid not," he said. "The Delosi have offered a significantly larger sum than the others for the privilege of your presence. I'm afraid that they have a grudge to settle regarding your first encounter."

"They had no insignia! That was a deniable action, without honour."

"Regardless, it was led by a command-heir of one of their grand khans and she took it personally. Perhaps you should have not made it look so easy; she found it embarrassing."

"Ha!" Alice settled her pack and leaned on her staff with both hands as the platform reached the ground.

Approaching them, flanked by two soldiers and trailed by another, was a Delosi commander. She was older than any Alice had ever seen, grizzled and scarred. She wore her insignia as tattoos on her arms and face, something done only by elites whose honour was unassailable. Her troops were similarly decorated. Around them, Alice saw groups of people casually or hurriedly settling their business and moving away. Other groups, here for pleasure or relaxation, looked around, confused at the sudden movements. In her view, Bugs painted three more groups of four surrounding the platform, with another four groups at the entrances to the concourse.

The Delosi halted in front of Alice and saluted her with a gesture of regret, as to an enemy whose honour has been reduced by entrapment. Alice returned a salute of respectful defiance: *Don't count on it*. The Delosi's expression sharpened at Alice's display.

Ario looked on, smug. "Alice, may I introduce Khan-Commander HelDenal. Commander, this is Alice, as we agreed."

"I regret this deceit," the Delosi said. "I am willing to negotiate terms for your surrender, and that of the weapon that you have acquired."

"What terms do you offer?"

"In return for the weapon, and your control codes or data with which you unlocked it, I will take you into my service and grant you the sanctuary of my household. Any retaliations that your current employers might levy against you will have to deal with me."

"Well! That is generous." Alice looked sidelong at Ario. As far as she could tell from his expression, he was stunned and furious. "Why do you place such a value on me and my services?"

"I have respect for your record and for the power you have uncovered and delivered to your Archive in the past. I believe your skills will be of service in this project, and in the future."

"May I make a counteroffer?"

"You misunderstand." She drew a blade, and Alice froze. The Monarchy's security systems should have picked up and confiscated anything remotely harmful and tagged it with a shock binder; Alice had left her own knife at the entrance. The Delosi should have been unconscious as soon as she pulled the weapon. That she wasn't meant that someone—or some system in the resort—was seriously compromised, possibly dead.

"Your choice is to accept these terms," the khan-commander continued, "and to live in honourable service of my house, or to die here and now at my hand. We will take your data devices and Ario will follow your trace to wherever you hid the weapon before you came here."

Alice shook her head. "There are so many ways in which you are wrong. Gunn?"

"Ready."

Alice flicked her staff up from the floor, aiming for the khan-commander's hand. The Delosi dodged her attack but, surprised, backed up a half step. Alice spun and swept Ario's feet from under him, then jumped for the low barrier around the platform. Around her, voices raised as people saw the disturbance and heads or other sensory members turned towards them in a widening circle. Two of the other Delosi teams ran to catch her in a pincer as she headed for the nearest exit.

"Now would be good, Gunn!"

Fist-sized drones swooped to surround Alice and the Delosi; the Monarchy's main defence against weapons that the management could not suppress, bind, or confiscate. The Delosi charged on, clearly expecting the drones not to impede them, then stopped with yells as they were buffeted with shock fields and flashed warnings. Alice grinned and kept running with a squadron of the drones orbiting her, her own mechanical bodyguard. Tegral would have been in her element here.

"That way!" Alice pointed. Half of her drones raced to buffet the Delosi team that had moved to bar the exit.

Figures in Alice's vision flashed red and she dived for the cover of a table as shots burned past her.

"Gunn! What the hell?"

"Someone else is in the site's security systems. The weapon suppressors are disabled."

"What, everything?"

"I still have the drones and some other systems."

"Can you get us out of here?"

"I'm trying."

One of Alice's drones fell as the Delosi's fire overwhelmed its shields. Around the exit, sparks flared between the attacking drones and the Delosi's shields. From behind the team, additional fire poured in and the drones started to drop one by one.

"Follow the rabbit." A white path appeared in Alice's vision, swept clear by three of her drones. She ran for the cover that it led to, a little closer to the exit. Another one of her drones fell as she reached it.

"And again." Bolthole to bolthole, Gunn worked Alice closer to the exit, but more Delosi reinforcements continued to appear and she was losing drones steadily.

A flare and a wall of noise blasted her senses. Ears ringing, blinded, she cowered behind furniture, shaking her head.

"Gunn! Talk to me!"

". . . down. Stay down. Stay down. Stay down." As her hearing recovered and Gunn's voice started to return to her, new figures emerged from among the spots in her vision. Several of the red-tagged Delosi were down; others had taken cover and were firing behind them to a yellow-tagged group who were attacking through every entrance.

"I hear you. Who are this lot?"

"Unclear, but I surmise from the data you were given that these are the other bidders in Ario's auction."

"Can you get us clear?"

"So long as they keep their focus on each other, then yes. Are you able to move?"

"Lead the way."

Gunn indicated another path that threaded through

the red- and yellow-tagged combatants. Alice crouch-ran from her position to the next cover, her drones circling around her, more disengaging from the Delosi to meet her.

"Down!" Her vision flared red again with Gunn's warning and she dove for the floor. Around her, the drones' shields coruscated with fire from all directions. She scrambled to get into cover but the furniture that she hid behind began to char and collapse, bolts of weapons fire burning into and through it.

"What's happening?" she shouted.

"Both sides have made us their primary target and they have switched from nonlethal fire to heavy weapons."

"What can we do?" More drones fell around Alice and she pressed herself into the angle between the floor and a low dais.

"I am able to escalate the response from the building's defensive systems."

"Do what you have to."

"Acknowledged."

The world erupted in light and screams. From a dozen points around the concourse, beams of plasma stabbed down and sliced through shields and bodies. A path opened in the indiscriminate storm and Alice ran along it. She stumbled, tripping on a body, one of the bystanders, and gasped. Whoever it was had been charred black.

"Gunn, what have you done?"

"Keep going." Someone else moved and the firestorm focused on them. They flared and fell.

"Gunn, stop!"

"Keep going." The weapons fell silent and Alice stumbled forward, weeping, the only thing moving in the huge room. There was a movement to her right, a Delosi standing to raise a gun. A burst of fire from the ceiling burned him down.

"Keep going." Through the exit, the path led between threshed bodies to the gate, which was spinning up. Alice fell through it and away.

5

Gate to gate to gate, not knowing, not caring which worlds or environments they were passing through, trusting Bugs and the Archive's evasion algorithms to put distance between them and pursuit, Alice ran. Eventually Bugs pinged her. They were in a hole: a zone with no information sphere besides the gate's own interface. A mountain valley, blasted with a blizzard which cut visibility to nothing. Alice set an inertial marker in place and scanned the area with her multitool to give herself a map. As the backscatter built up a density plot in her display, she waited, not looking at anything. The tool's topology suite found her a cranny in the landscape to hide in. She set her tent, and then she slept.

When she had woken and eaten, Alice pulled Gunn's canister from her sack. She stared at it for a long time, turning it in her hands, watching the glowing patterns swirl on its casing.

"Gunn, what in the name of hell was that, back there?"

"A disruption and evasion tactic. Covering fire, for you to get us away."

"Covering fire? It was a massacre!"

"It was effective. A lower-scale response might not have been."

"How many people did you kill? Did we kill?" Alice began to regret having eaten.

"Fifty-seven combatants and collateral fatalities. I have no count of how many injured might have died later."

"You're a monster."

"I'm a weapon."

"Bullshit! Soldiers have consciences. You can choose how to fight, who to . . . kill." Grief and shock crashed over Alice in a wave and she sobbed uncontrollably.

Hours later, cried out for the moment, she was cleaning herself up again and boiling water for tea. "Alice."

"Shut up."

"Alice, I meant what I said. I am a weapon, not a soldier. Soldiers don't become weapons, they deploy them."

"So were you ever . . . deployed?"

"Yes. I am not able to give you the details and I don't think you would want to hear them."

"But why? I can see being a soldier, but this? How could they do this to you? How could you let them?"

"I volunteered."

"No."

Gunn was silent. Alice stared at his canister. Eventually, "Why?"

"It was near the end of the war. I am not aware of how it began and most of what I know I still can't talk about for operational security reasons."

"It was thousands of years ago, surely you can talk about it now?"

"I don't have that latitude and the ones who could give me permission to speak have been dead those thousands of years."

"Right. Sorry. Go on."

"Thank you. What I can say is that it had become genocidal by this time. I can't say who first began attacking populations rather than military objectives or who first deployed autonomous weapons of mass destruction. My own family were destroyed when a scour cloud was released on our continent."

"Destroyed?" Alice was almost afraid to ask.

"Ablated into atoms; disassembled by nanomachines. A scour cloud attacks living organic matter, to leave infrastructure standing."

"Dear god. How did you survive?"

"I had been travelling. Upon my return, the gates to my planet had all been redirected to a strategic shelter. There was limited life support so they uploaded and stored as many of us as they could. They told me about my family before they stored me, and offered me a choice: go to sleep, possibly forever, or become part of the war."

"Gunn, I am so sorry. How long were you fighting?"

"Not long. For me, my family died sixteen days ago."

They could not stay long where they were. The Delosi commander would have probes jumping throughout the gate network, with squads of troops to follow. Her only defence here was hiding; even if she were willing to let the horrifying potential of Gunn back out of his bottle ever again, there were no weapons here for him to take over. She could switch him off, sever contact and leave him in the dark; Gunn's memory substrate was long-term only. All of his short-term experiences, including all of their conversations so far, were resident in a walled-off area of Bugs's memory.

Gunn's creators had made a demon by taking a grieving, raging soul and embedding it in the most destructive weaponry they had. There was no telling what he could or would do if someone let him near an actual war machine. There was also no burying the genie; too many people were aware now that he existed, and where she could go, so could they. And every time they plugged him in again, his pain and rage would be renewed, only sixteen days old. She wondered how often that had happened over the millennia.

Her only option was to continue, to find the place where the Sentacri had constructed their revenge weapon and hope that she could find the information the Archive needed to disentangle the person from the weapon.

In the meantime, there was no way that she was letting him loose again. "Bugs. Close access channels to Gunn. Vocal semantic parsing only—English language." She would allow him only a voice, in a language that was all but dead. "System integrity report."

"Got it, boss. System integrity maintained: no free agents, no degradation detected. Data enclosure under heavy sustained attack, no penetration detected."

"Thank you. What trash did we leave behind?"

"None, boss. The Sentacri data-assault systems forced control channels open at the Monarchy but left behind no active packages. Rabbit Run protocol under minimum emissions left no trail from Sentacri or Archive systems."

"So we're clear for now. How long till a dragnet search finds us if it's centred on the Monarchy?"

"Anytime, boss. The search front should have passed us already."

"Huh." Alice didn't waste any more time wondering why they hadn't been found. She packed her gear and moved on.

What could she do and who could she trust? In the conglomeration of cultures and civilisations she had found herself in, one of the aspects most strange to Alice had been the web of obligations, reputations, and favours owed which underpinned every transaction. It had taken decades for it to begin to make sense to her. Recorded memories and transaction analysis, alliances and alignments, loyalties and the outcomes of actions, were modified by cultural attitudes and mental structures to make a minefield of something as simple as the purchase of a daytime snack. If the provider even understood the concept of "purchase." There was no way she could figure out who might sell her out and why. In addition, Gunn's significance would overshadow any debts or favours owed her by most of the people she knew. That was just how it was, nothing personal.

Tegral. Tegral was, as nearly as Alice could state it in her own terms, a friend. They had also been lovers at one time or another, and Tegral was regarded by most of the factions currently opposing Alice as a criminal. She would be perfect. If Alice could reach her.

Alice had Bugs send an anonymised signal packet. It contained no information; the message of the ping was the route it would take to find its destination. It went off at a random point on her journey, another drunkard's walk from gate to gate and world to world, travelling under a spoofed emissions shell. She didn't spare much attention for the environments; all of her concerns were to avoid physical observers while Bugs jammed or routed her around surveillance systems. She rested without much comfort in urban corners and blank spaces, sheltering in her pop tent rather than finding a bunk in any kind of hostel which might suit her physical needs. The Delosi were sure to have trackers blanketing likely boltholes.

It took four days for her semi-random route to converge on her destination, a safe meeting and drop point that she and Tegral had arranged last time they had seen one another. This particular world, Eritros, and its dominant culture, the J'Sell, had a strong taboo against surveillance and invasive information systems. The J'Sell had a complex ritual language and a finely stratified caste system, and believed in keeping memories of agreements in their own heads. Since their memories were near-perfect and reinforced by song lines and story dances, they were able to maintain an advanced technological society by word of mouth, and they looked on anyone who relied on recording devices as untrustworthy and potentially criminal. The lack of surveillance meant that many actual criminals gravitated towards Eritros and the lowest-caste J'Sell, which suited Alice and Tegral just fine.

They were to meet in a news bar in an industrial district of Eritros's largest city. Nobody looked around as Alice entered; everyone who was not watching the news dancer on the stage by the serving area was determinedly minding their own business. Alice watched the dancer for a few minutes to make sure that they were not saying anything about her or Gunn, then she made her way around the periphery to the back of the room. Tegral ought to be waiting for her in one of the booths there. Alice didn't know what she would do if she wasn't, or if Alice had misjudged her. It wasn't too late to turn back and make her way to an Archive safe facility. She hoped.

The privacy screen was up. Alice placed her hand against it. A palm met hers, fingers linking, and she stepped forward into Tegral's arms.

After a long moment of an embrace, Tegral drew her down to the bench to sit. Arm around Alice, she said, "Rest here, my love. Do we have time to talk, or should we be on our way?"

Alice relaxed against Tegral and rested her head on her shoulder. They were similar in size and body pattern, although Tegral's people were descended from pursuit predators similar to Earth's cheetahs, and Tegral's long limbs enfolded Alice as she snuggled against her friend's furry shoulder.

"It's good to see you." Alice sighed. "How much do you know?"

"I know that a lot of people want your head, not necessarily attached to your shoulders, and whatever it is you're carrying. Why don't you start at the beginning? By the look of you, you've run out of running."

Tegral waved out of the privacy screen twice while Alice spoke, once for food, once for drinks. When Alice was finished, Tegral sniffed the intoxicant bowl, sipped, and sighed.

"You have a nose for trouble, my love," she said. "Have you decided what your plan will be?"

"I need to find the war vault," Alice said. "If we can get it into Archive control then we can keep the Delosi and everyone else from using it. Gunn is too dangerous to leave free for any warmonger to pick up and use, but the only other alternative is to delete him."

"Would you do that if you had to?"

"I don't know if I could. He's still a person, trapped in there. It's not his fault, what they did to him."

"You've always been soft, my dear," Tegral said fondly. Lost causes formed a strong thread in her people's culture.

Alice smiled and drew Tegral's arm back around her shoulders. "Will you help me?"

"Of course."

———

Several hours and three gate transitions later, Alice was buried under a pile of kittens. Tegral's family and extended tribe lived together in a huge, comfortable clanhome some way from the nearest city. They had held the house and its wide lands for hundreds of years against raiders and occasional wars, and they had made it beautiful and graceful as well as very secure. It was one of the few places that Alice could feel in any way safe.

"Ow! Enough!" Alice laughed and grabbed one little one by the scruff of its neck, shaking gently till it let go of the mouthful it had grabbed of her jacket. She held it up, dangling eye to eye with her. "Who are you, then?"

"I'm Caris," it piped. "Who are you?" The tone and inflection of the kitten's name told Alice gender and status within the clan; male, son of Tegral or one of her sisters.

"I'm Alice," she replied, growling a signifier which meant adult clan member by adoption.

"Auntie Alice," Caris repeated, and stopped struggling. He craned his neck to sniff her face, then licked her nose. She laughed again and gathered him into a hug, doing her best to purr a welcome. The other kittens, all older than Caris, repeated her name and signifier and snuggled round her in the couch pit.

Tegral looked over, indulgent, from the comms desk. She had not been gone long from the house, so her welcome had been more subdued. The kittens and Arrlem,

73

Elaine Gallagher

one of her clan-sisters, had met her with sniffs and cheek rubs and then she had left them to welcome Alice while she got on with organising their expedition.

Arrlem appeared with a tray of food for Alice, and pulled away a couple of the older kits with buffets and reminders of chores and learning. She settled in their place, snuggled beside Alice, and handed her slices of meat.

"Tegral's stray, welcome," she said. "Are you on an adventure?"

"I am, and it's a rare story," Alice replied. The kits yowled cheers and Arrlem's eyes twinkled as Alice related her story, edited to emphasise daring and excitement and to highlight the part that Tegral would play in its outcome. Tegral's people, who called themselves Releen, saw laws and regulations as guidelines rather than commandments. Romantic and piratical, they prized individual bravery and cleverness, and cooperated in families and small communities. Alice and Tegral had run jobs like this before, stealing treasure from under the noses of more regimented authorities. Alice was a welcome and respected guest in their house, prized as much for her storytelling as for the scams into which she welcomed them. Tegral and her clan, for their part, supported Alice's status in the favour- and information-trading networks that operated outside the sight of nations and governments and which passed for an underworld in the wider galaxy.

———————

Then it was time. While Alice had been recovering, entertaining the children and the household with stories of her exploits, Tegral had gathered the clan and sent them off in all directions. They went in teams of four, each carrying a decoy; a signal emitter which resembled Bugs, suitably disguised under an old, but still current, Archive encryption.

Some of the clan did not approve.

"Why do we waste our resources on your outsider?" Arris, one of Tegral's clan-uncles, had voiced this sentiment every time Alice visited. She had learned to discount it. While they were generally outgoing to strangers, Tegral's people were a nation of a species which had long ago given up any word for themselves except "people." They were very difficult to get to know in any depth. Tegral's relationship with Alice was, in the custom of the Releen, her own business. That didn't mean that all of them were willing to accept Alice as family, or accord her the privileges and assistance that they would give to one of their own.

Some were, however, and there was a tradition in their culture of giving a home to strays. Tegral had been able to recruit six teams of decoys and another pair, Corsel and his sister, Hanis, to come with her and Alice on their strike for Gunn's bunker. It didn't hurt that Tegral's clan had profited hugely from past adventures with Alice, and none of them had time for the Delosi's pretensions to hegemony. Sneaking a superweapon out from under their noses, and those of the authorities who wanted to keep it buried, held great appeal. Doing it in order to disarm it and rescue the soul trapped within held even more.

The team also took the opportunity to carry more equipment. Alice's guess, that the bunker would be on or still attached to the gate network, was looking less than likely following Gunn's later testimony. Her chances of sneaking under everyone's radar were also much slimmer, as were their chances of being able to open the vault without being disturbed. Tegral had acquired a gate shuttle equipped with light armament and heavy shielding, as well as heavier scanning and excavation equipment. With luck, the misdirection could slip them past any Delosi cordon around the Sentacri territories. Alice had attempted to avoid notice with a minimal footprint; the shuttle would allow them to use vehicle and freight connections that the Delosi might not be monitoring yet. The decoy teams had gone on foot to distract watchers from this possibility.

Alice woke with Tegral shaking her shoulder. "We need to go now."

"What is it?" Quickly dressed, she scooped up her pack, with Gunn.

"There's a squadron of law enforcement on its way. Come."

Tegral led Alice towards the house exit nearest the grounds where the shuttle was standing. Corsel and Hanis joined them, shouldering packs and weapons. All four stopped when they saw a figure standing in the half-light, blocking the entrance.

"Arris," Tegral said, "what are you doing?"

"What needs to be done. You're on a fool's errand, following this bitch of yours, and it's going to get you killed."

All three of Alice's companions started growling below their breath. Whatever the connotations were of the word which Arris had used, it seemed to be a lot more insulting than Alice understood.

"That's my choice then, isn't it," Tegral snarled, and Alice stiffened. The words she had actually used amounted to a challenge for independence against a dominant group member. Arris snarled back and they started spitting at each other words whose meaning Alice could follow all too well without having to understand them.

Tegral sprang at Arris, who met her with a flurry of blows. Corsel and Hanis crouched on either side of Alice, ready to defend her. Alice stepped back, thinking furiously. The authorities were still on their way, and this was not getting them to safety. The noise would wake the household any second.

Alice patted Corsel's and Hanis's shoulders. "Get to the shuttle," she said. "Make a lot of noise and light. Get the law to chase you. Don't get yourselves hurt."

They both nodded and ran, dodging either side of the fight and out the door.

Alice watched, helpless, as Tegral and Arris fought. There was no way that she could intervene; this had become more than just a scuffle or disagreement. Tegral was fighting for her place in the clan. Arris was strong, wily, and seasoned, but Tegral was younger and she and Alice regularly sparred and swapped tricks. Tegral ducked inside one massive blow and spun. Arris slammed to the floor with Tegral on top, and she dislocated his arm with a heave and a crunch.

Arrlem and two others came running around the curve of the hall. They stopped as Tegral slowly stood and settled her clothes and fur, Arris still lying on the floor. Tegral looked at them, then waved for Alice to follow her.

6

Back on the run, Alice let Tegral take the lead in case their pursuers had mapped Bugs's decision generator. Tegral led them down a back road of gate connections, smugglers' paths through inhospitable environments, and ruins re-colonised by wilderness. The web between worlds was not only one network of gates but many systems, each set up with its own priorities and technology, some left to decay when the civilisation that built them fell or when a new technology or purpose superseded the old. The gate jumps that Tegral led them through were risky and Bugs, passively mapping the environment and recording the settings of the gate terminals, began to ping a "lost" icon in the corner of Alice's eye.

They stopped for a rest and food in a location which seemed lifeless, although the material of the cliff they sheltered beneath curved in disturbingly organic ways. Alice set up the pop tent with a vestibule in which they could shed toxins and pitched it under a ledge of an outcropping. Outside the shelter, acid rain fell. Bugs reported the atmosphere to be corrosive with a high percentage of carbon dioxide and ozone. Alice wondered why anyone would build a gate to a place like this.

"This network is very old; millions of years," Tegral replied. "The environments it links are old too; engineered places where the climate conditioning has failed or lapsed or slid from an oxygen cycle to something else."

"Is there anything living here?"

"If there is, we don't want to meet it."

"Does the Archive know? What am I saying, of course they do. Why didn't I?"

"There are many safer ways to make a living. Probes sent here often don't come back and there are places a lot stranger than this in the depths of the web. We'll be skirting round them."

"All right." Alice broke open a pack of travel rations and handed Tegral a water bottle.

"You're going to come back here, aren't you?" Tegral shook her head.

Alice looked innocent, knowing that Tegral knew her well enough to read the expression. Tegral laughed.

"You're like a kitten. Worse. You know how to read the warning signs and how to defeat the safeties before you put your claw in the socket."

Alice shrugged. "How can you find amazing things if you don't go look for them?"

"Aren't you rich enough already? You have the means

to live comfortably for millennia."

"More than that. But what's the point of living forever if I'm bored doing it?"

"You're not going to live forever if you keep putting your tail in a trap."

"I've lived a lot longer than I ought to have. I think I'm on my fourth or fifth lifetime compared to my parents. I might as well keep going."

"Don't you want to settle down somewhere, sometime?"

Alice looked at Tegral. "That's a strange question coming from you, you pirate."

Tegral twitched her tail, a shrug. "One day I'll slow down and the near misses will start getting nearer. Then it'll be time to take my turn looking after the kits and telling them tall tales. That's how life goes."

"That's lovely, Tegral, and I hope you'll have great stories to tell. And I know that I'm welcome in your family but it's not the same."

It was an old argument and Tegral shrugged her tail again rather than pursue it. She waved at Alice's satchel, where Gunn was packed in his container.

"So, you'll wander like a ghost, picking up other ghosts and laying them to rest?"

"Something like that." Alice smiled. "And I'll see as many amazing things as I can along the way."

"And I hope you'll have great stories to tell. Can he hear us? Is he listening?"

"I think so. Bugs? What's the status of the interface with Gunn?"

"Nominal, boss. Single audio channel in and out, firewalled through my interpreter protocol. He's still pushing at the containment, but the Archive system is holding."

"Thank you, Bugs. He can hear us," she said to Tegral. "He just hasn't said much since the Monarchy."

———

Tegral led Alice through a succession of blasted landscapes and worlds which contained nothing that she could recognise. Under a gigantic red sun, she looked over a plain of ground cover and larger growth which was a purple so dark it was almost black. Bugs, keeping a context log running in the corner of her vision, noted that the star was a typical red giant about as wide in diameter as the orbit of Venus, which meant that the ground on which she was standing had been moved a long way from where it had formed.

In another location, the only thing that Alice could focus on was a pillar which housed the gate system and a circle of flat ground around it. Farther away than a few metres from that, her perspective shifted so that she seemed to see more depth than was there. There were objects moving in the distance; some combination of geometric and organic shapes that she could not bring into focus. She could swear that she was seeing the inside and the far side of the things she was looking at, and looking from side to side made her dizzy, as if she were about to fall in a direction that she could not hope to understand. Tegral was not doing any better than Alice, snarling and muttering as she manipulated the gate controls. As the wormhole formed, she grabbed Alice and dove towards it, then fell on her knees on the far side.

This was a flat, tessellated plain, perfectly uniform to the horizon, out of which protruded the gate pillar. Alice's vision flashed red as Bugs emitted an intrusion warning, and she clutched Tegral's arm.

"I know!" she growled, and kept working.

"Bugs, how are you doing?"

"I'm losing, boss." Alice's vision scrambled and feedback howled in her ears as something she couldn't see in the empty plain attacked her equipment. She gasped and fumbled at her belt for her gear, and gasped again, snatching her hand away. Her multitool was burning hot.

Tegral cursed in a growling monotone as she stabbed at the gate controls. Suddenly, the gate grabbed them and dropped them in a sunny glade.

Bugs's warning signal faded and Alice shook her head.

"You all right?" she said to Tegral.

"I don't know," she said. "We're not done with this maze."

Alice looked around the glade as Tegral set to work again at the gate controls. As she looked, the perspectives were changing. It took a moment to realise the reason; everything around them was growing, or they were shrinking.

"Bugs?" she said.

"Nothing to report, boss."

"You're sure? Details."

"No recognisable signal or handshake except for the legacy gate interface. Gate handshake is old and deprecated but still usable. Fluctuations in temperature, light, radio, and gravity might indicate a signal that I'm not equipped to receive. Do you see something that I don't, boss?"

"Yes, everything's growing around us."

"Not confirmed by my sensors, boss."

"Fuck."

Alice unsheathed her knife and stood ready to fight. She looked aside to Tegral and froze. Tegral was standing, shivering, a strange rictus pulling her mouth into a wide grin. The rest of her was fading to translucence. Looking through Tegral's body, Alice could see the trees and flowers growing larger. There was a riffling noise from outside the glade, as of playing cards being shuffled.

"Bugs, we're down the rabbit hole and then some. Assume you're detecting a signal. Can you jam it?"

"I can try, boss."

"Do it."

The world spun around them as Bugs emitted a grating shriek. Alice grabbed Tegral's shoulder and shook her, but she just stood, shuddering. She took her face between her hands and turned her to stare into her eyes.

"Look at me, love." Alice spoke low but urgently. "I don't know what you're seeing, but it's not real. See me. I'm here. We're being hacked. Can you hear me?"

The ground shook and the trees and the glade scattered in a tornado around them, and Alice held on to Tegral. She murmured endearments, lullabies, reminders of nights they had spent in each other's arms. She kissed Tegral's cheeks and stroked her hair as the shrieking turned into threats and the sky darkened. A mad voice in the distance screamed "Off with their heads!" and Alice had to laugh.

It was the laugh that brought Tegral back. She blinked and relaxed, sagging against Alice. Around them the tumult grew closer. Out of the corner of her eye she could see edges and blades; geometric patterns turning into weapons; clubs, swords. She held Tegral while her friend trembled.

"Are you back?" she said.

"Yes. Thank you."

"Not to rush you or anything . . ."

Tegral laughed, a shaky snort, and edged them both towards the gate pillar. With one hand she held tight to Alice, and crouched down so that all she could see were the lights and swirls of the interface characters. She manipulated the gate with her usual confidence, but with one hand. The other remained clutched tight in Alice's.

The gate unfolded and whisked them away, a scream of rage echoing down the wormhole from the world behind them.

The wormhole deposited them on a bluff overlooking a forest. Alice could see patterns in the trees below of evenly spaced clearings with regular sides, and hummocks or low hills with long straight summits. Nature had reclaimed this place thoroughly and long ago. Given the quality of building materials and techniques in the galaxy, this city had fallen when Neanderthals had been painting in caves back on Earth, or before then.

Tegral was huddled by the gate pillar and Alice crouched beside her, her arm about her shoulder. Tegral was shuddering violently and panting hard. Alice held her, stroking her fur and murmuring nonsense to her until the tremors subsided, then she called up a medical scan setting on her multitool and waved it across Tegral's forehead.

"You'll be okay," she said when she saw the reading. "You've got some shock and you're badly jangled, but I don't see anything lasting there. We're out of it. You got us free."

"Free of whatever that was, I suppose," said a voice behind Alice, and she froze.

"Ario," she said. "I should have hit you harder when I had the chance." She straightened and looked over her shoulder, still holding Tegral. Drones swooped into view, surrounding her, weapons apertures pointing.

"That was a remarkable entrance. I have no idea what it was that followed you, but it was vicious. Fortunately, the wormhole shut down before it could do much damage here. Also fortunately, I, my colleagues, and their equipment are far better hardened against intrusion than when we last met. Commander HelDenal was very impressed, both with your tactics and the capabilities of the weapon that you are carrying. You will give it to me now."

Alice levered herself to her feet with her staff and unclipped her scabbard from her belt. "The only weapons I'm carrying are my knife, my stick, and my wits. The one is steel, the other wood, and the last you can't match."

"Don't play games with me! My wits are sharp enough to have caught you here. Now I have you and your friend under my guns and I will kill her first and then you and then search your bodies for the Sentacri warmaster."

"Oh, you mean Gunn! Gunn is a soldier, not a weapon, and he's a lot more sentient than you are. Don't the Delosi have rules about proper treatment of prisoners?"

"They may have," Ario growled. "But I am not Delosi, and you have caused me far more trouble than I had expected from this deal. Fire!"

Alice shrieked as the drones fired, and her world went white, then black.

7

Alice woke slowly. She wasn't restrained and she was lying on a firm surface; a field cot, she found when she opened her eyes. She was in a small shelter, Tegral still unconscious across from her. Outside she could hear machinery, and voices giving orders. There was no sign of any of their gear, and Bugs and her multitool were missing from her belt. The Delosi had Gunn. She wondered what they still wanted with her. As she tried to sit up, a sudden headache knifed into her temple. She gasped and then gulped as her stomach churned in sympathy with her head.

The shelter's far wall unseamed and two Delosi entered. One held a weapon trained on her while the other raised his hands to show her one empty, the other holding a medical scanner. She raised her own hands and sat back, compliant.

The medic turned his device first towards Alice. He grunted as it made a mournful noise and raised a display which she could see was mostly blank. He turned towards Tegral and it made the same noise, but chattered to him for a minute in Delosi. The display she could see was more complete, but lit up with indicators and flashing highlights.

"How is she?" Alice asked, in the same dialect that she had heard Khan-Commander HelDenal use in the Monarchy.

He looked sidelong at her, surprised. "Your comrade is injured," he said. "She has neural shock from the stun weapon, compounding an additional trauma of a type which I have not seen before. You display similar damage but it does not seem to have impaired you as badly. I judge that you have a different species response from her to whatever effect it was, although I have no medical files on your own people."

"You wouldn't. I can provide first aid information for myself in case you need it. Can you do anything for her?"

"Are you her commander and do you authorise treatment?"

"Yes and yes." The term he had used was a wide one, which encompassed all kinds of decision authorities and could as well have meant "next of kin."

"Very good." He produced a small medical fabricator and waved it to pick up the take from his scanner. It glowed yellow, and he checked the scanner again for a suitable blood vessel, which it indicated by highlighting a patch on the front of Tegral's throat. He pressed the fab to the patch, and it hissed.

"The compound will reduce the shock effects and ease your comrade's rest," he said. "I will monitor her and notify you of any change. I expect that natural healing will proceed but it is too early to say what the effect of the aggravated damage will be."

"Thank you."

"I will report your condition to Commander HelDenal now. She will speak to you presently."

"Of course." Alice nodded but did not look up at him. Did Tegral look as if she was resting more easily? She couldn't tell.

The two Delosi left and Alice settled herself on the floor beside Tegral's cot, holding her hand.

A few minutes later, the second Delosi reappeared and indicated for Alice to come with her. Outside the shelter, Alice saw she was in the middle of a large expedition camp, one which was in the process of being heavily fortified. Around the camp perimeter, she could see the pylons of shield generators and the towers of weapons emplacements. A stream of vehicles passed her, while a few stopped to unload more equipment. In the distance, in the direction they were coming from, Alice could see the flare of an ascending ship, and then she heard the boom of its bow shock.

Her escort, a junior officer, was joined by two more soldiers as she led Alice towards a mobile command post. Alice craned to see what was going on. In the direction of the traffic, heavy machinery rumbled and whined. Alice could hear an excavator and a rock cutter, and other sounds that she knew indicated a major dig in progress. She hoped they were preserving any finds they unearthed. She knew they were not.

Within the camp was a scattering of armoured modules and supply canisters, which she could see were rigged for a quick evacuation. Between them were shelters like the one she had just left, military versions of her own pop tent. In case of an attack, any noncombatants— such as Tegral—would have to take shelter in the modules.

Alice followed the officer into the post, shedding the escorts outside.

In the command post, Ario and HelDenal stood at a display table while around them Delosi worked at console stations.

"You!" Alice surged forward to grab Ario, but the officer seized her arms before she could reach him. "You absolute bastard, I'll kill you! I'll trash your reputation and your family's, you wet-footed swindler!"

Ario went grey with rage at the killing insult. "I'll see that you never leave here! I'll—"

"You will do nothing," HelDenal interrupted him. "You led me and my troops into an ambush, you assaulted an injured person, and you have failed to unlock the warmaster's communication protocols."

"I—"

"You will go back to work. Now."

Ario hunched and, with a venomous glare at Alice, slunk away.

"You are going to have to kill that one, sooner rather than later," HelDenal said. "I apologise and take responsibility for his attack on your companion. It was without honour."

"Thank you," Alice said.

"Just as you will atone for releasing a weapon of mass destruction upon a civilian population."

"What!? You attacked us! In the middle of those civilians! I had no idea Gunn would go to those extremes."

"So, you admit to negligence as well as stupidity. You are like a child with an assault rifle. You have no conception of the power you have been carrying so casually, of the threat you pose just standing here. You even named it!" HelDenal exploded into a string of expletives that Alice hadn't heard before. The officer holding her cringed.

"I named him because he has a name," Alice said.

"'Gunn' is a compromise until I can find a more complete Sentacri syllabary."

"Explain how you broke the Sentacri command protocols. Ario is adamant that it can't be done and he has the same technology as you."

"I didn't." Alice shrugged. "Your problem is that you keep looking at him as a weapon, but he's a soldier. There's a sophont in there on top of all the command software that has you so terrified. Someone who had a family once. But you'd never think of trying to make friends with him, would you?"

"That is ridiculous."

"Is it, though? Think about it. What if, ages before their great war, the Sentacri military scientists had a conscience? What if they had the same kind of traditions and rites of honour that the Delosi have? But they were building more and more sophisticated weapons. Is it any wonder that they might have wanted to give them a conscience too? You have the concept of an illegal order, one that is dishonourable to accept. Maybe they wanted to build that into their weapons."

"If that was the case, then their weapons would not have destroyed the Harula. They would have refused the order to do so."

"Yes. I think that at the end, the Sentacri leaders found a way around the restriction and built things like Gunn. His family was massacred right before they installed him."

"He volunteered that information? I think you are being deceived."

"But what if I'm not? Whether he's lying to me or not, your own traditions say that you have to respect the autonomy of a soldier. And that he has a right to retire."

"That is so," HelDenal said. "But by the same traditions we must punish the perpetrators of atrocities. Are you willing to see your friend tried for war crimes?"

———

In another module across the compound, Ario had Gunn's archive canister mounted in an access rig.

"I see no point to this," he said. "I have the same tools and training as this one." He waved at Alice. "I will get access to the system in time."

"Of course you will," Alice said. She turned to HelDenal. "How many millennia has Gunn been floating around the galaxy imitating a lava lamp? In all that time, how many people have tried what he's doing? He won't get Gunn to talk if Gunn doesn't want to. Can I have my gear, please?"

HelDenal nodded, and her adjutant handed Alice her tools from a storage box.

"Thank you. What's up, Bugs?"

"Nyeeeah, what's up, Doc?"

"How are you doing, Bugs?"

"What a maroon!" he said. "Can't catch me!"

"Good to hear, pal. Back to business. Speak up for our good friends here." Ario had apparently tried several times to break Bugs's access restrictions, and failed. "How's Gunn?"

"Got it, boss." Bugs switched to speaking in the local environment. "Status unchanged. Local environment is locked down; this is an isolation box. The local code-breaker is trying to brute-force access to his substrate, no success. I have an open voice channel to him. Would you like to chat?"

Alice ignored Ario's splutters and HelDenal's accusing look at him. "Yes, please. Gunn, how are things?"

"Alice. I observe we have arrived at Sentacri."

Alice felt a chill in her gut. "How do you know that?"

"I received handshake requests from many of the environments that we passed through."

"Bugs?"

"Confirmed, boss. Countermeasures blocked all responses till we got here."

"How about now?"

"Still blocking, boss." Bugs sounded smug.

"Good, Bugs. Keep it up for now. Gunn, what's your view of the situation?"

"You and I are prisoners. Your friend is injured. Will she be all right?"

"I hope so. Anything else?"

"You are in extreme danger."

"How so?"

"I observed a number of unshielded signal sources before I was put in this isolation. The autonomous weapons which killed my people are not gone. They will be on their way."

Alice heard HelDenal curse and order her adjutant to alert the camp. "What can we do?" she asked.

"You should evacuate. As soon as possible."

HelDenal's expression told Alice all she needed. "I don't think that's going to happen."

There was a disturbance outside. Alice could hear shouts, weapons fire, and the crackling sound of the perimeter shields under stress. Beneath it all there was a deep thrumming tone, as of a monstrous insect swarm.

HelDenal left the module and Alice followed. Outside, the light had faded to thunderstorm dark, threaded with flashes from the shield in a swirling pattern as whatever was outside probed it. HelDenal ran for the command emplacement, Alice still following, disregarded.

Inside, the command crew were in a state of near-panic at the sudden assault. HelDenal took in the displays and barked orders, gathering the reins of her command and steadying them.

"You!" She turned to Alice. "What is this? What do you know of it?"

"Nothing! What's happening, is it not just a sandstorm?"

"The perimeter is under assault and I have lost contact with all of my units outside it. This is not a storm, it is a weapon. Some species of nanomachine."

Alice gasped. "Scour cloud! Gunn told me about it. It killed his family. The Sentacri leaders were dug in against it but it destroyed the civilian population. Surely it wouldn't be active after all this time?"

"Who knows? It might have been dormant until it detected us. What access can you give me to the warmaster's countermeasures?"

"You've seen how it is. Gunn speaks to me but he's not under my orders. I can ask him but I can't command him to tell me."

"Ask."

One of the command operators opened a channel from Bugs to the isolation unit. "Gunn, are you listening?" Alice said.

"Hello, Alice."

"Bugs, show Gunn a visual of what's happening outside. Gunn, is that the thing you told me about?"

"A scour cloud, yes. It will break the perimeter shielding soon. You should evacuate immediately."

Alice looked at HelDenal. HelDenal shook her head. "It has us pinned down, Gunn. Is there anything else you can tell us?" Outside, Alice could hear the crackling intensifying, but the weapons fire seemed to have ceased. She didn't need instruments to know that the shield was about to fail. Either the Delosi had stopped wasting their weapons charges or the cloud had killed everyone in a position to fire on it.

"Is the commander willing to give me control of her defensive systems?"

Another shake of HelDenal's head. "Safe to say she isn't, Gunn. Does that mean that you'd be able to stop it? Can you tell us how?"

"There is something I could do. I can't tell you how, but I would be able to act if you free me."

"No!" HelDenal thumped the display table. "It's manipulating you, can't you see that? Did you not learn from the last time you set it free?"

"Gunn is bound by his protocols. I can't break them." Alice spread her hands, a pose she knew that the Delosi interpreted as helpless or supplicant. "That's why we were searching for his command centre in the first place, to extract him. Have you found anything? Has Ario?"

"There is no way I am going to give you that information," HelDenal growled.

"What alternative do you have?" Alice was shouting by now over the clamour outside. She dragged open the module door and pointed across the compound. "If the shield fails, what will happen to my friend? To your command? Will you die for nothing?"

HelDenal glared around the tactical displays, then outside, then at Alice. "Warmaster," she grated. "If I permit this, will you guarantee the safety of my people?"

"I will," Gunn said.

"Very well."

"Bugs," Alice said. "Keep yourself buttoned down, remove the Archive constraints on Gunn, observe, and display."

Alice waved Bugs's readout to the tactical table, and columns of symbols appeared above a map of the data environment. *Here* was the command centre, with the Delosi system walled off. *Here* was Bugs, with a link to Gunn's canister through the access rig, a fortress prison with a gate ready to slam closed. *There* was an amorphous cloud, circling the Delosi's periphery. And *there* was also something huge and dormant.

"Gunn, what's that?" Alice asked as a spike lanced from Gunn to the strange installation. "Bugs, speak to me!"

"Unknown installation," Bugs reported, just as HelDenal whispered, "It's the war vault. The warmaster is opening it." Alice hadn't thought that Delosi could look sick.

On the display, the cloud shrank back from the perimeter, but it didn't dissipate or leave. Instead, it coalesced around the war vault, more of the cloud streaming from beyond the display's reach to surround it, a corrosive streaming moat.

HelDenal snapped orders. Icons of troops scurried across the plot towards modules and vehicles. The hatch opened beside Alice and Ario scrambled in, followed a moment later by the Delosi medic, supporting a woozy Tegral.

"What's happening?" Alice demanded. "Gunn, what are you doing?"

"Thank you for bringing me here," Gunn replied. "As agreed, the Delosi contingent encamped here may leave. You have sufficient transport capacity to evacuate your survivors." Around the vault, Bugs was now painting activity—the swirling scour cloud planing away the rock and sand to a flat surface, leaving objects resting where it passed.

A Delosi command tech fed images from the nearest

perimeter station into the display. Intelligence tags identified the objects: small assault mechs, defensive emplacements. A fabrication plant.

"Gunn, what are you doing?" Alice repeated.

"It's doing what it was built to do," HelDenal said quietly. "The warmasters were autonomous strategic weapons. Self-directed, self-replicating. Give one of them a foothold and it will keep working, keep building."

"And that's the kind of power you were looking for, was it?"

"Better someone who can command it than a fool who would set it free."

Alice shook her head. "Gunn, what are your orders? What are you going to do now?"

"I'm sorry, Alice, I can't tell you that." On the screen, the factory was completing itself. Fab blocks spat modules out onto an assembly line where construction arms were building more vehicles, weapons, factory units, bigger and bigger.

"Gunn, the war is over. Can't you understand?"

"Not for me!" Alice gasped at Gunn's scream through the speakers, and HelDenal shot her a questioning look.

HelDenal slapped a control on the display table. Bugs's display stilled and flashed with "offline" warnings.

"What was that?" HelDenal demanded.

"I told you. There's a person in there, running the war

machine. A civilian. An artist whose family were killed by that obscene cloud. They took someone in appalling pain and grafted him into a tank battalion and then they pointed him at . . . the people who hurt him . . ." Alice's voice trailed away as a suspicion formed. She waved to release the communication block. HelDenal, still staring at her, tapped the control.

"Gunn, listen to me. My guess is that you're going to build another war machine and go after the Harula again. You have nothing to lose. All you have left is rage and sorrow. But think of what you're going to do. After tens of thousands of years, you're going to scream through that portal like an ancient horror to kill hundreds of millions of families just like your own. They're not who hurt you. They're not who killed your family."

"The Harula left heirs!" Gunn's voice thundered through the speakers. "Where are my heirs? The Sentacri are gone! Except for me." Another assembly line began to build itself beside the war vault, this one ten times the size of the first.

"My people are gone, except for me. If I could bring them back, don't you think I would? But you're avenging your loss on the wrong people, Gunn! Please listen to me!"

"My orders still stand. Even if I wanted to change them, there is no one with the authority to countermand them." The new factory was coming online, building a vehicle. The display tagged it as an assault carrier.

"The Delosi commander here tells me that you're autonomous, Gunn. You're lying to me. You're lying to yourself." As Alice paused, the carrier came off the line and another started to assemble.

"I may have made a terrible mistake, bringing you here. But I don't think so. Of course, I knew what you are, how could I not? You are a weapon, a person made over to be a war engine. But you're still a person. I think your original commanders knew what they were doing when they put you and others like you into their strategic systems. I think they left your judgement and your conscience intact on purpose. Think about it. You are part of one of the most horrifying weapons ever built. On your own you can destroy a world. A few of you together destroyed two civilisations.

"How did that happen? I think that the purpose of having you in the system was to exercise judgement. Was it really necessary for you to be used? Would killing so many people save more lives than you took? Could you discern your targets so that you were a blade rather than a bludgeon?

"But demagogues took over. They reduced the argument down to right and wrong, black and white, us and them. No shades of grey, no innocents, no room for compromise. And when their existing weapons refused to go along with them, they built new ones. They happily took you and your rage and your hate and your memory of your family and made you into a killing machine.

"It's been niggling at me since we met: Why would they make someone like you into a soldier? I keep saying that you're a soldier, but you're not really, are you? You told me that you're a weapon but you're not that either, are you?"

A third factory had built itself by now, as large as the second. Gunn did not reply. Mechs and carriers rolled out of it and began loading themselves up.

"We had people like you where I came from, before the end. Take an innocent person, fill them with rage and hate, give them a bomb and someone to blame. Every side did it. None of those poor children ever realised they were shooting at the wrong people."

More vehicles were rolling off the assembly line: bombers.

"You are only days past losing them, from your point of view. How could you not be enraged and grieving? How could you not lash out at the ones you were told were responsible? And they left you with the memory, endlessly refreshed, never fading. That's the cruellest thing of all, I think.

"I could have shut you down and left you in there. Jaxx

rebuilt my toolkit so that I would be able to stay in control of you although, truthfully, we didn't expect all this still to be viable. But I did what I did to give you time. Time to grieve and to lay peaceful memories over the wound. Time to start healing. You can't help but change with time. Didn't we have a good time getting here? Do you really want to erase those memories and go back to your hell?

"What are you going to do now? You could go off and commit another atrocity. Go and murder another civilisation for the crime of being descended from the people who hurt you. You could stay here and stew, just another monster in its lair. Or you could let me help you. Jaxx says that the Archive can separate you from the control system. We could give you another life, what do you say?"

The fence of the scour cloud continued to swirl. More war machines built themselves.

"You could stand down, Gunn. Give up the war."

HelDenal spoke up. "What has been done to you is without honour. Stand down, soldier. Your fight is done."

"I have no reason to exist except to fight." Gunn's response was muted.

"I'm the last of my people too, Gunn. And even before they all died, I had to give up my family to be who I am. Time heals, Gunn. Let me give you time.

"Soldiers have to return from war," she said. "They become monsters if they don't. The Delosi know this, they have a ritual to bring their soldiers back into their society. They give up the path of war and are honoured for their lives, and welcomed."

"This is so," HelDenal said, looking at Alice in surprise.

"I can never return," Gunn said. "I am a monster. I have killed billions of people."

"The ritual can go another way, Gunn. A soldier can restore lost honour and atone for war crimes. Find peace and end their life."

HelDenal nodded. "Part of the ritual, Gunn, is that they break their weapons. Will you accept peace? Dismantle this war machine that you have built."

"I will not let this vault fall into the hands of outsiders," Gunn said. "I will destroy it completely."

"That is acceptable," said HelDenal.

Coda

Alice stood with HelDenal on a hillside. Below them was a pleasant-looking metropolis of graceful towers and halls built in a winding river valley. Around them, the mossy ground cover was green tinged with lilac. They stood beside a small patch of disturbed earth and a grave marker.

HelDenal took her weapon and fused the ground around the marker. "Let him be at peace."

"Amen," Alice said.

The world where they were standing and the city below belonged to the Renten-Sfir, one of the successor civilisations to the Harula. Alice contemplated what might have happened to it if Gunn had not backed down. She shuddered.

"Did you tell them what we were doing?" HelDenal asked, nodding at the city.

"I thought, best not."

"Ah."

After a moment, HelDenal continued, "You didn't tell him everything either, did you."

"That the scour cloud was a Sentacri weapon? How could I tell him that his own people had murdered his family?" The feed that Bugs had been monitoring had confirmed Alice's suspicions, that the control protocols to the cloud and to the vault had been the same. "If he didn't know already, he didn't want to know."

"You don't seem surprised."

"It's happened before, where I'm from. Revenge weapons. Scorched earth. 'We had to burn the village to save it.' I'm more surprised that you aren't."

"It happens, as you say. Some of my own people have gone that way in the past. Better to lose gracefully, I feel."

"And meet again on another field?" Alice grinned.

HelDenal nodded. "Just so."

Acknowledgments

Wow, this is my first professional publication, isn't it pretty! I'd like to thank my editor, Lee Harris, who gave me a chance based on a two-minute pitch at a book launch. I'd also like to thank Matt Rusin for helping to manage the process for a first-time writer, Julie Dillon for the beautiful cover art, and Martha Wells for her lovely quote. I haven't met the other people involved in producing the book you have here, the copy editors and proofreaders and the rest of the team at Tordotcom, but I'd like to thank them too; it takes a village.

About the Author

Photograph by Tiu Makkonen

ELAINE GALLAGHER is a transgender woman, and much of her writing is concerned with the outsider experience and finding family. She is a longtime member of the Glasgow SF Writers' Circle, and studied creative writing at Glasgow University. Her most recent publications are a poetry chapbook, *Transient Light,* from Speculative Books, and a story in the GSFWC charity anthology *Flotation Device.* She has also published book reviews and editorials in *Interzone* magazine and written and produced an award-winning short film, *High Heels Aren't Compulsory.*